Bedtime Snuggles

WITH CHRISTOPHER

By Barbara Davoll

PICTURES BY DENNIS HOCKERMAN

MOODY

With love to my Roy, who is always there
for me when things go "bump in the night"

All Scripture quotations, unless otherwise indicated, are taken from the *Holy Bible, New International Version.*® NIV.® Copyright 1973, 1978, 1984 by International Bible Soiciety. Used by permission of Zondervan Publishing House. All rights reserved.

Scripture quotations marked KJV are Taken from the King James Version.

Printed in the United States of America

TABLE OF CONTENTS

BEDTIME SNUGGLES

"Christopher, it's time for bed. Come put your toys away,"
Mama said in loving voice. "You've had a busy day."

Christopher looked up at her, his lips were in a pout.
"Please, can't I play some more? I just got my soldiers out."

4

"I tell you what," said Mama. "Let's play a little game.
I'll help you march your soldiers home, if you will do the same."

"That will be a lot more fun than playing by myself.
Let's march them down across the rug and then onto their shelf."

So Christopher and Mama began to put away
His little soldiers in their place for fun another day.

"And now, my little soldier, let's march you to the tub;
Here's soap, a towel, and washcloth; your body needs a scrub."

"Christopher, you're splashing me! Don't get it on the floor!"
laughed Mama as she hid behind the churchmouse bathroom door.

"Now it's time to get you out," said Mama standing by;
"Brr! It's cold!" said Christopher. "Hurry up and dry!"

With a sniggle and a giggle, "I'm hurrying," Mama said.
"I'll help you get your nightshirt on and tuck you into bed!"

"But Mama, do I have to? My bed's a lonely place;
Besides that, I don't like the dark," he said with tearful face.

6

Mama Churchmouse picked him up and carried him to bed;
"I didn't know you feared the dark," the concerned mother said.

Sitting on his bed with him, she wiped away a tear;
"Snuggle up and share with me what causes you to fear."

"It's when you blow my candle out," Chris said in shaky voice.
"I think there's something in my room; I sometimes hear a noise."

"Let's blow your candle out right now," said Mama for a test.
"I'll stay in here, and we will see what's keeping you from rest."

So Mama blew his candle out and stayed right by his bed.
Just then they heard a little thump. "That's it!" Christopher said.

"Oh, that is just the furnace, when it is cooling down.
And when it starts to burn again you'll hear another sound."

"I'm so glad to know that's it," said Chris with great relief.
"I thought someone was in here, maybe a crook or thief.

"Mama, there is something else I'd like to ask about;
Do you see that big black thing that is moving all about?"

Chris was pointing 'cross the room; something sure was moving.
His mama hugged him close and said, "That's your curtain blowing."

"How funny!" said the little mouse. "Of course, now I can see.
The curtain that is blowing there was what was scaring me!"

Just then they heard a footstep upon the little stairs.
"Here's Papa now to tuck you in; you know how much he cares."

"Why, Chris, it's past your bedtime," said Papa in surprise.
"I'm not sure that staying up is smart or very wise."

"Mom and I've been talking about my bedtime fear.
But now I'd like to talk to you, seeing you are here.

"Papa, I don't like the dark when I can't really see;
I guess that I imagine things are where they shouldn't be."

"I can understand, my son," said Papa, sitting down.
"I wish it didn't bother me," Chris said with a big frown.

Papa thought and then he spoke: "There's nothing you should fear.
Mom and I are here close by; now wipe away that tear."

"Just think about the nighttime as a special time of day,
when God is wrapping up the earth and putting it away.

"His little creatures scurry home to their warm beds and nests;
the twilight seems to call to them to find their homes and rest.

"Little children kneeling down beside their beds in prayer
ask the Lord to watch and keep them always in His care.

"Like you they are protected, watched over from above.
They trust in their Creator God and His unfailing love."

10

Chris smiled up at Papa. "Now you may tuck me in.
And if I have another fear, I'll talk to you again."

Papa kissed his little son and then to Mama said,
"I think he'll feel much better now and like to go to bed."

They softly tiptoed from his room and left their little mouse,
and not another creature stirred within the churchmouse house.

TUCK-ME-IN TIPS FOR PARENTS

Bedtime fears of children are normal and usually stem from their worry of being separated from the rest of the family. This is accentuated if their bedrooms are upstairs and some distance from where the rest of the family is spending the evening.

Christopher's Mama wisely handled Chris's reluctance to get ready for bed. By making a game of putting his soldiers away, Mama avoided a clash of wills with her little mouse. Playing "soldier" and "marching" to the tub further extended his play time and made it enjoyable.

When she discovered Christopher had some genuine fears, she listened and analyzed them, showing her care for him and helping him find a solution. It was obvious that both mouse parents had a nightly ritual of "tuck-me-in time." Letting the child know a few minutes ahead that bedtime is near is very helpful. This and a set bedtime each night helps a children to know what to expect. Soft Christian music on tape and a night light can help bridge the time when they go to bed and fall asleep.

Christian parents have the wonderful opportunity to make bedtime a very special time to read God's Word and instill His truths of protection and watch care over our little ones. It is especially comforting to tell them that the Lord never slumbers or sleeps (Psalm 121:4) but is always watching over them in loving concern. Committing them to the Lord in prayer wraps them in God's love and allows them to rest in the knowledge that He is in control of all that concerns them.

BEDTIME BRAVERY

Bedtime bravery is being able to go to bed happily anywhere, trusting in the Lord to protect you from harm.

"I will lie down and sleep in peace, for you alone, O Lord, make me dwell in safety." (Psalm 4:8)

CHRISTOPHER'S BRAVERY HAT

Christopher, wait for me," puffed Mandy Churchmouse. She ran to catch up with him as school let out. "That was so brave of you to climb up the high ladder and get Miss Tilly's scarf out of the tree. I would have been scared to climb that high. How did you do it?" she asked.

"Oh, it wasn't much." Christopher shrugged. "I just put on my pretend bravery hat and didn't look down. I thought it was nasty of Sed to tease the teacher that way. It made me embarrassed that he's my cousin."

"Well, he's nothing like you," said Mandy with admiration. "You're nice to everyone—and brave too."

Christopher felt his face growing red from her praise. He knew he wasn't really very brave. *But at least I was today,* he thought with happiness.

Later that evening Christopher went to his grandparents' house to stay all night, because Mama and Papa Churchmouse were away. After having some fun playing games, Christopher took the

little candle they gave him and went upstairs. He wasn't used to going to bed all by himself. At home, Mama and Papa always tucked him in.

As he walked up the stairway, the candle made shadows on the wall. *That looks like a bear,* he thought, shivering. But he kept walking. He didn't want Grandpa and Grandma to think he was a big baby and frightened.

When he got to the guest room, he undressed quickly and hopped into bed. *I should blow out the candle now,* he thought. *But it will be so dark, and I'm alone.* Just then he remembered what the teacher had told the boys and girls in Sunday school. Christopher had been listening behind the door. The teacher had said that God the Father was always with them and that they were never alone.

I guess that means He's with me too, thought Christopher. *Even if I'm just a little mouse He's watching over me.* With that thought and a smile on his face, Christopher blew out the candle and snuggled down happily. *I'll have to tell Mandy I put on my pretend bravery hat again tonight too,* he thought as he drifted off to sleep.

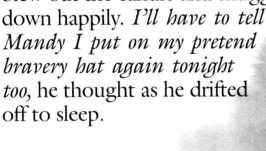

SOMETHING FOR YOU TO THINK ABOUT?

1. In Ephesians 6:17 we are told to put on the "helmet of salvation." That is kind of like a bravery hat, isn't it? If we have Jesus in our hearts and lives, we can think about Him and ask Him to keep us from all harm.

2. Have you asked the Lord Jesus to come into your life? The Bible tells us in Romans 10:13 that "whosoever shall call upon the name of the Lord shall be saved." If you have not done so, why not do it now? When you do, you will have on a real "bravery hat"–the "helmet of salvation."

NO FRAIDY CAT HERE!

Sometimes at night when I'm alone
And have a little fear,
I just put on my bravery hat:
There's no Fraidy Cat here!

For when I think I'm all alone
I know it isn't true.
Jesus wipes away each tear:
There's no Fraidy Cat here!

A BEDTIME PRAYER TO PRAY:

Lord Jesus, sometimes I am afraid at night. Please help me to trust You to take care of me always. Help me to learn to go to sleep happily anywhere. Thank You that You are always right beside me, guarding and keeping me through the night. Thank You for loving me so much. Good night, Jesus.

PATIENCE

*Being patient means waiting happily for something you want,
with no fussing or complaining.*

*"For whatsoever things were written (before) were written
for our learning, that we through patience...might have hope."*
(Romans 15:4 KJV)

ONE MORE TRY!

"Here comes a fastball, Chris. Get ready!" Freddie Fieldmouse squeaked. The little mouse got set to throw the ball.

"I can't hit fastballs, Freddie," complained his friend Christopher Churchmouse. "Give me a slow one. I can hit those."

"Nope!" Freddie shook his head. "If you always do the easy balls, you'll never get better. It takes really fastballs to help you become a good player. Here it comes!" True to his word, the fastball zinged over the plate. Christopher swung and missed. "See! I told you," Chris yelled.

Freddie hitched his cap and set himself for another fastball. He was determined that he would help his churchmouse friend improve so that he could be a member of the team, not just a substitute. The mice boys were hot and dusty when they trudged home.

"Whew! My arms hurt," complained Christopher. "I feel awful."

"Yes, I know. But it won't hurt for long. I think you're getting better at hitting, and your catching is very good," Freddie insisted.

"Aw, I think I'll just quit. I'll never be as good as you are," moaned Christopher. "This is too much like work."

Freddie stopped and looked at his friend. "Look, Chris, you're getting better. It will be worth it when you're a full team member. I know you. You aren't a quitter. You'll make it," he encouraged. "Just be patient."

"I guess you're right, Freddie," replied Chris. "I'm not a quitter—but I sure could use some of your patience."

"Yeah, well, I just lost it. I'm getting *very impatient* for supper!" Freddie said with a laugh. "Let's hurry home!"

SOMETHING FOR YOU TO THINK ABOUT

1. It is hard work to become a good ball player, isn't it? Can you think of something that is hard for you to do?

2. Ask the Lord Jesus to give you patience to keep trying. Remember, He loves you and will help you with everything in your life.

CHRISTOPHER'S POEM ABOUT PATIENCE

You need a lot of patience
When you're learning to tie your shoe;
You need a lot of patience
When you are learning to glue.

You need a lot of patience
When your sister has broken your toy;
You need a lot of patience,
Whether you are a girl or a boy.

You can't buy it at the store;
It's not inside a trunk
Don't look behind the door
Or underneath your bunk.

There's one place you will find it—
In the Bible tucked away;
There you'll find your patience,
If you'll only read and obey.

A BEDTIME PRAYER TO PRAY:

Lord Jesus, help me to happily wait for all the things You want me to have. May I be quiet and patient and not complain when I have something hard to do. Thank You for being patient with me when I do things I shouldn't and for helping me learn patience. Amen.

20

CHEERFULNESS

*Cheerfulness is putting on a happy face, even when you don't feel like it;
it's letting the joy of Jesus shine through you.*

"Rejoice in the Lord alway: and again I say, Rejoice."
(Philippians 4:4 KJV*)*

PENELOPE'S VISIT

"Hey, Mandy, what's the matter? Your face is long enough to eat peanuts through a picket fence." Christopher Churchmouse sat down beside his friend, who was looking very sad.

"My mama just told me Cousin Penelope is coming for a visit, Chris. She is going to stay for a whole month! And I can't stand her! She's always breaking my toys and getting me in trouble. She acts like a princess and expects me to wait on her."

Mandy dropped her voice to a whisper. "And she lies too. She really does. She just says anything she wants, whether it's true or not."

The little girl mouse lowered her head and pouted. Then she began to cry. "I don't want her to come."

Christopher patted her shoulder awkwardly. "Aw, cheer up, Mandy. Pouting won't help. I know she's a pain. The last time she was here, I was ready to turn Tuffy the cat loose on her. But it will be all right. It's only a month, and I'll help you get through it. So will Sed, Ted, and Ned. We're still your friends, aren't we?"

"Yes, but I don't want her to break my toys," she said. "And I don't like her telling lies." She was pouting again.

Chris thought for a minute. "I think I have an idea. Let's bring all of your special toys to my house and leave only the things you don't mind getting broken. Then it won't matter. And about the lying, remember the story of Pinocchio. Every time he lied, his nose grew."

Mandy giggled. "Christopher Churchmouse, you know that's just a story!

"Right! And that's what her lies will be. *Just stories.* Nobody will believe her, Mandy. We all know you. Her lies can't hurt you. But that long face of yours can. You might trip on your lower lip," he said jokingly.

Mandy threw back her head and laughed. Christopher always made her smile. He was such a special friend. And he was right. Pouting never helped anybody.

"Let's go get my favorite things and move them to your house before Princess Penelope arrives," she said with a giggle.

She knew now that she could stand having Penelope for a month. Christopher would help her smile through it.

SOMETHING FOR YOU TO THINK ABOUT

1. What was making Mandy so sad?

2. How did Christopher help his friend Mandy? How are some ways you can be more cheerful?

A SMILE JUST WAITING

Have you ever noticed
that just above your chin
There's a smile that's waiting,
If you'll only let it in.

There among the freckles
that seem to take up space,
There's a smile just waiting,
If you'll notify your face.

When you're sad and feeling blue,
there's something you can do:
Take that smile that's waiting
And put it to work for you.

'Cause when you've got an attitude
and think you'd like to pout,
Don't forget a smile is waiting
To bring the sunshine out.

A BEDTIME PRAYER TO PRAY:

Lord Jesus, sometimes I don't feel happy, and I forget to be cheerful. Please help me not to pout. Help me to remember Your joy and let it shine through me. Teach me to be cheerful, I pray, and encourage others who are feeling sad. Good night, Jesus.

RESPONSIBILITY

Responsibility is knowing what you are supposed to do and doing it in the right way and at the right time; it is a lot like being dependable.

"Whatever you do, work at it with all your heart, as working for the Lord, not for men, since you know that you will receive an inheritance from the Lord as a reward." (Colossians 3:23–24)

PAPA TAKES A FALL

Christopher Churchmouse was doing his homework. Miss Tilly had asked the class to write each of their spelling words five times. *This is taking a long time,* the little mouse thought. *I think I'll just write them three times. I'm sure Miss Tilly won't count them. She just wants to be sure we know them for our test tomorrow.*

Christopher knew he would make a good grade on his spelling test. He always did. *Why should I sit here and write these out?* he thought. *I'll do fine tomorrow, I'm sure.*

Just then there was a terrible noise in the kitchen.

"Oh no! Christopher, come quickly! Your Papa has fallen down the basement stairs," squeaked Mama Churchmouse. "Hurry! He may be hurt badly."

Christopher jumped with fear. He ran to the basement stairway and looked down. There was Papa, lying on the floor at the bottom of the stairs. Mama was bending over him.

"Papa! What happened?" The little mouse hurried down the steps.

"I'm all right, Chris," said Papa weakly. "I slipped on that hammer and fell all the way down the steps. It's funny, I don't remember even using the hammer."

"Now, dear, you just lie still," Mama fussed. "We'll get your brother Rootie to help us carry you upstairs. I hope your ankle isn't broken."

Chris stood by watching. He had a sick feeling in his tummy. A big lump came up in his throat, and tears stood in his eyes.

"Papa, I'll go get Uncle Rootie, but there's something I have to tell you first." The little mouse hung his head in shame. "I didn't mean to, but I left that hammer there. I used it, and I was going to put it away. I meant to—but Freddie called, and then I forgot. I'm so sorry." And he began to cry.

"It's all right, Son," said Papa kindly. "I know you didn't mean to cause this. But you must take some responsibility. I've told you time and again to always put things away when you use them."

"Yes, and you've also been told *never* to put things on the stairs," said Mama sternly. Chris knew she felt bad about Papa and wanted Christopher to remember the next time. "Now please go get your Uncle Rootie so we can help Papa upstairs."

Later that evening, as Papa was resting comfortably in bed, Christopher finished his homework. He was careful to write each spelling word five times, just as Miss Tilly had asked. He had learned a hard lesson that evening about the meaning of the word responsibility. Doing his homework correctly—and on time—was another way of being responsible.

SOMETHING FOR YOU TO THINK ABOUT

1. What caused Papa Churchmouse to fall down the stairs? What should Christopher have done with the hammer when he finished using it?

2. Can you think of some ways you can be more responsible? What are they?

MEANT-TO LAND

There is an awful land,
Where all the things you planned
Never are followed through,
Things you meant to do.

It really isn't fair
Our meant-to's are caught there.
We meant to take a stand
But went to Meant-To Land.

"Put off another day,"
We hear old "Meant-to" say;
And time is too soon past–
Meant-to's never last!

If we could know the cost
When Meant-to's all are lost,
I'm sure we'd take a stand
Far off from Meant-To Land.

A BEDTIME PRAYER TO PRAY:

Lord Jesus, I need to be more responsible. Help me to learn this. Teach me to always be trustworthy and dependable like You. I love You, Jesus. Thank You for loving me even when I forget to be responsible. Amen.

PRIDE

To have pride in your life means that you have an over-high opinion of yourself or that you think you are better than others. Another word for pride is vanity. A person who is vain thinks only of himself.

"A man's pride brings him low, but a man of lowly spirit gains honor."
(Proverbs 29:23)

A NASTY SURPRISE!

Several mice children from the Mouse Hollow School were gathered around the hall bulletin board. They were looking at a list of names that were posted.

"Are the names there of the kids who won the music scholarship?" asked one of the mice girls who was standing on her tiptoes trying to see.

"No, Miss Tilly hasn't put them up yet," Christopher Churchmouse answered. "But I can tell you who will win," he said with certainty.

"Aw, come on Chris. You don't know who won," scoffed his cousin Sed. "No one does. Miss Tilly said it would be a secret until she puts up the list of winners."

"Oh, well, of course, we'll have to wait for the list, but it's obvious who won," he continued smugly.

"Tell us, Smarty, if you know so much," teased another mouse.

"Well, everyone knows that Melinda Mouse will win the girls' scholarship, and I will win the boys'. I mean, what other boy has taken piano as long as I have?" he asked proudly.

Mandy Churchmouse, Christopher's very special friend, dropped her head. She had never seen her friend act like this. She was ashamed of his acting so proud.

30

"You do play pretty well, Chris," agreed Freddie. "But that new mouse in third grade is supposed to be good." Freddie was also ashamed of his friend's being so boastful.

"Have you heard him?" asked Christopher.

"Well, no, but others have and–"

Just then their conversation was interrupted by Miss Tilly. "Hmm. Wonder what you're waiting for?" she teased, as she pinned the list to the board.

As Miss Tilly stepped aside, the mouse in front of the crowd gave a long look and then a whistle. "Surprise! Surprise!" he said.

Pushing his way to the front, Christopher looked at the list and suddenly felt sick. The new mouse had won! Christopher turned and headed for home with tears stinging his eyes. He could hear the laughter behind him.

Why did I act like that? he thought. *It wouldn't be half so bad to lose if I hadn't said I would win. How will I ever be able to face them again?*

SOMETHING FOR YOU TO THINK ABOUT

1. What made Christopher think he was going to win the music scholarship?

2. Do you have something you do well? Who gave you the ability to do it?

A CASE OF VANITY

Did you ever get the feeling
That you are the best?
Bigger, smarter, cuter too
Than any of the rest.
If you do, you'd better look out,
For it's sure without a doubt
You've a case of vanity.

Oh, vanity and pride
Are things you cannot hide!
For everyone knows
Your vanity shows;
It comes from deep inside.

When you're feeling you're the best,
There's something you can do;
You can to the Lord confess,
And He will humble you.

A BEDTIME PRAYER TO PRAY:

Lord Jesus, please help me to remember that I must humble myself before You. Help me not to be proud about anything but to realize that all I am and all that I have is from You. May I have a humble and meek spirit like You. Amen.

HONESTY

*Honesty means always telling the truth, no matter how hard that is.
It is being fair and trustworthy in all we do.*

"Truthful lips endure forever, but a lying tongue lasts only a moment."
(Proverbs 12:19)

THE MOUSE HOLLOW FIELD TRIP

There was a lot of excitement in Mouse Hollow School. Tilly Teacher was announcing the names of the mice children who would get to go on the special field trip next week. All the mice held their breath, hoping they would be selected. Only the mice who had the highest grades could go. There would be room on the little mouse bus for just twelve students.

"I know I won't be going," said Christopher Churchmouse glumly. "I really messed up on the reading test."

"Well, you never can tell," said his friend Freddie Fieldmouse. He wanted Christopher to go very badly, as they always had such fun. They both knew Freddie would be going for sure. He always made the highest grades in the class.

The teacher began to read the list. "Freddie Fieldmouse will be going, along with Sed, Ted, Ned, Mandy, Christopher, and–"

"Christopher! You made it," interrupted Freddie. He grabbed Chris and began to jump up and down with excitement. Freddie was so excited that he was pounding his friend on the back. But Christopher did not seem happy.

"Chris, what's wrong?" asked Freddie. "Aren't you glad you're going?"

"I'm not going, Freddie. There's been a mistake. I know what I made on that test. There is no way I can go."

"Aw, sure there is. Miss Tilly said so. Now be happy. I just know it's–"

"There's been a mistake, Freddie. I've got to talk to Miss Tilly," said Christopher, starting toward her desk.

34

"Class, I need your attention," said Miss Tilly as Chris went back to his seat. "Christopher has been honest enough to point out that he did not do well on his reading test this week. Therefore he does not qualify to go on the field trip after all. Danny Dormouse will be going instead. I really appreciate Christopher's honesty," finished Miss Tilly.

Chris sat quietly in his seat, blinking back the tears. He felt terribly sad because he really wanted to go. But he knew it would not have been honest. *Perhaps next time*, he thought.

SOMETHING FOR YOU TO THINK ABOUT

1. What did Christopher do that was very honest?

2. Can you think of some time when you were not honest and should have told the truth? Confess that to the Lord Jesus and then tell your parents or teacher about it. You will feel so much better for being totally honest.

A BIG PACK OF LIES

If you should tell a lie today,
You're in for a big surprise.
That lie will grow and grow and grow,
Until it is a big pack of lies.

The lie you tell to your mother
Will be followed by another;
And right before your very eyes
Will grow HUMONGOUS in its size!

There's only one thing you can do;
And that's to tell only what's true;
You'll never be caught if you do what is taught
In the Bible just for you.

A BEDTIME PRAYER TO PRAY:

Lord Jesus, sometimes I am not totally honest and forget to tell the truth. Help me to always remember that You want me to be truthful in all my ways and words. Help me to know that You are the Truth. May I always live by Your Word. Amen.

LOYALTY

To be loyal means that you are a true and faithful friend and always believe the best. It means you will stand up and defend your friends, even when others turn away.

"A friend loves at all times, and a brother is born for adversity [or to help in time of need]." (Proverbs 17:17)

THE STOLEN SKATEBOARD

"Hey, Mandy, wait for me," called a little girl mouse as Mandy left school for the day.

"Did you hear about Christopher Churchmouse stealing his cousin's skateboard?" she asked.

"What are you talking about?" asked Mandy with a frown. "I haven't heard anything like that. I'm sure it's a mistake. Christopher would never take anything that didn't belong to him," she stated firmly.

"Oh sure, I knew that's what you'd say. You think Christopher is a Goody Two-shoes. But I heard this from Sed Churchmouse himself. He told me that he saw Christopher take Ted's skateboard from the playground and roll away on it. He said Ted is really upset!"

"I'm sure that isn't true," Mandy insisted. "Christopher would never do that."

"Can you prove it? Bet you can't," taunted the other girl mouse.

"Well, I don't think it happened— and I will prove it," stated Mandy. With that she flounced away and headed for the Churchmouse home.

When she got there, Christopher wasn't home. "I think he's riding his new skateboard," Mama said.

Mandy's eyes got very big and round. She didn't know Christopher had a new skateboard. He hadn't said a word to her, and he usually told her everything. *You don't suppose he did take it?* she began to think as she started down the street. But she quickly rejected that thought. *No way!*

Just then a fast blur came around the corner, nearly knocking her down. As she caught her breath another blur headed for her. This time the blur did knock her down. "Hey, watch yourself, Ted! You knocked Mandy down!" Christopher yelled, jumping off the skateboard and helping her up.

Looking at him curiously she asked, "Where did you get that skateboard, Chris?"

"Oh, Grandpa Churchmouse bought it for me for helping him rake leaves. It's just like Ted's." He laughed, watching Ted skate away. "Except I don't knock girls down on mine."

"Well, that's a relief," said Mandy. "I heard..."

"That I took Ted's? Yeah, I know. Sed thought that, too, until he saw us together with our boards. It was a good joke on him. You didn't believe it, did you, Mandy?"

"Not for a minute," Mandy said. *I knew I'd prove it,* she thought happily.

SOMETHING FOR YOU TO THINK ABOUT

1. What did the little girl mouse tell Mandy about Christopher? Why do you think Mandy didn't believe her?
2. Where did Mandy go to find out if it was true?

MY VERY SPECIAL FRIEND

I have a very special Friend
Who is always loyal and true;
This special Friend believes and loves,
No matter what I do.

Unlike some other friends of mine
Who may turn and walk away,
This special Friend will stay nearby
No matter what I say.

Although I have some earthly friends
Who are loyal and kind and true,
Jesus is my heavenly Friend,
And He'll be your Friend, too.

A BEDTIME PRAYER TO PRAY:

Dear Jesus, I thank You for my friends. Help me be loyal to them and always think the best of them. Please help me to choose friends who love You, and may I be a friend that brings joy to them. Thank You for being my best Friend. Amen.